Stephen Mackey

Miki

and the Wishing Star

Hodder
Children's
Books

A DIVISION OF HACHETTE CHILDREN'S BOOKS

Moonshine, starlight and falling snow,
Watch how the magic begins to grow.
Wishes and dreams — will they ever come true
For Miki and Penguin and Polar Bear, too?

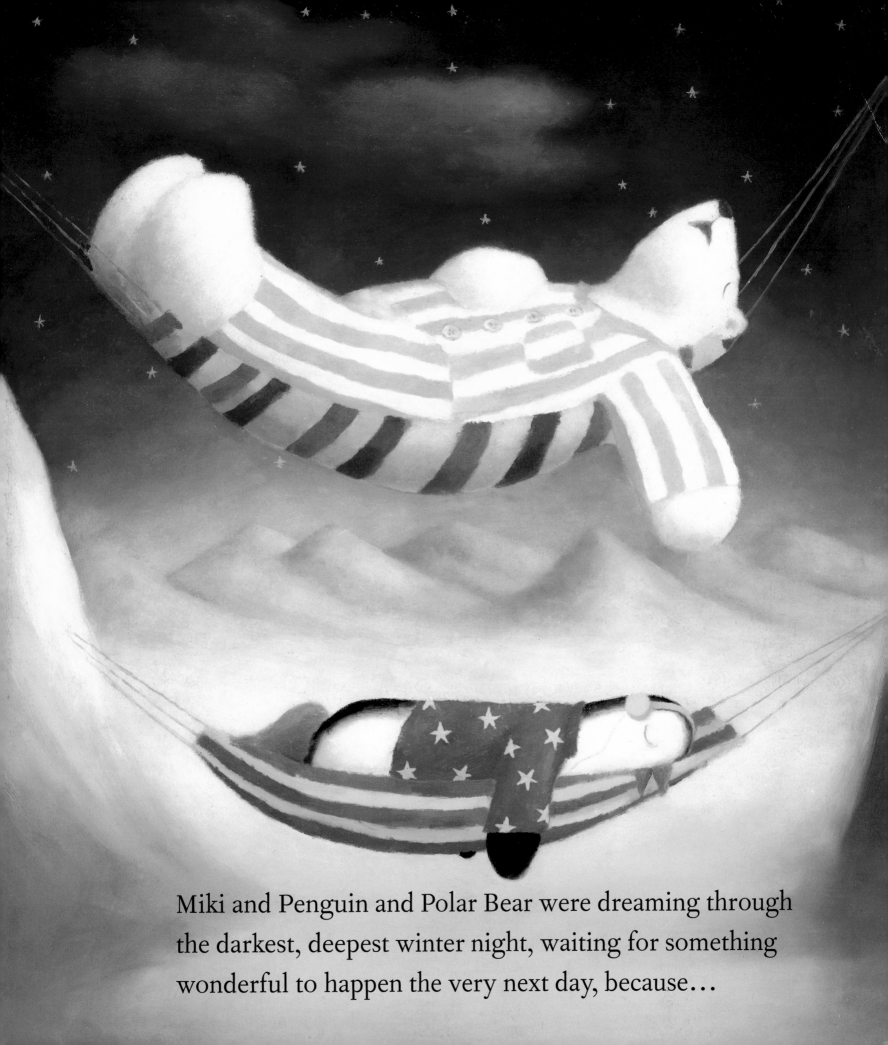

Miki and Penguin and Polar Bear were dreaming through the darkest, deepest winter night, waiting for something wonderful to happen the very next day, because…

...it was their birthday!

'And because it's *everyone's* birthday,' said Miki, 'we can *all* have a wish when we blow out the birthday cake candles.'

'Me first! Me first!' squeaked Penguin.
And he closed his eyes and wished a very secret wish.
'I wish I wasn't so very small.
I wish I was the biggest penguin of all!'

And way up in the cold dark sky,
a wishing star burst into a million tiny crystals of magic.

And Penguin got his wish.
'Where is he?' cried Miki anxiously.

'I'm up here!' laughed Penguin.
'And I'm the biggest penguin in the world.'

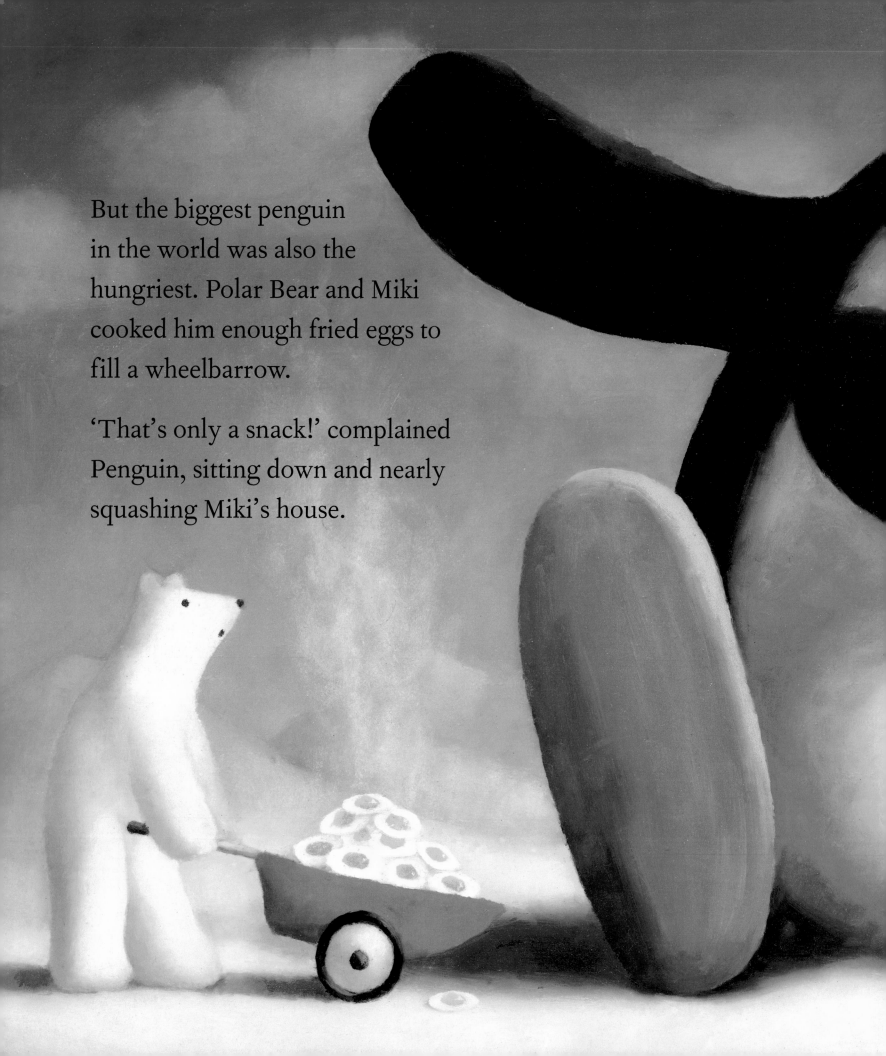

But the biggest penguin
in the world was also the
hungriest. Polar Bear and Miki
cooked him enough fried eggs to
fill a wheelbarrow.

'That's only a snack!' complained
Penguin, sitting down and nearly
squashing Miki's house.

'Then you'll have to find breakfast somewhere else,' said Miki.

'I WILL!' said Penguin.
He stomped off, singing:
'I'm the biggest, I'm the best —
I'm much BIGGER than the rest!'

Before long, he met a crowd of scared little penguins marooned on an ice floe.

'Penguin to the rescue,'

he cried, making a bridge.

Then he wrestled with sea monsters!
He really was a big brave penguin.

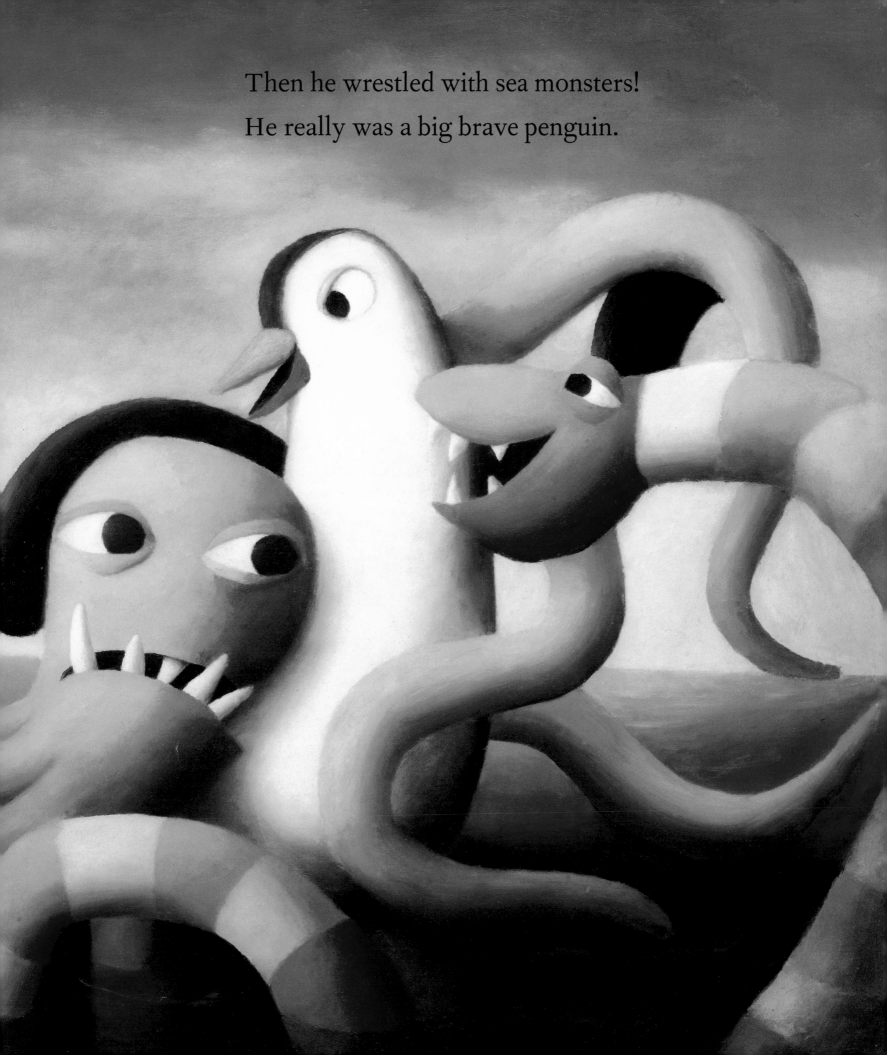

But Miki and Polar Bear were very worried. Would Penguin ever come home again?

Polar Bear used his birthday wish straight away.

'I wish our Penguin now to see
exactly as he used to be!'

And, far, far away the wishing star exploded into countless enchanted splinters of ice.

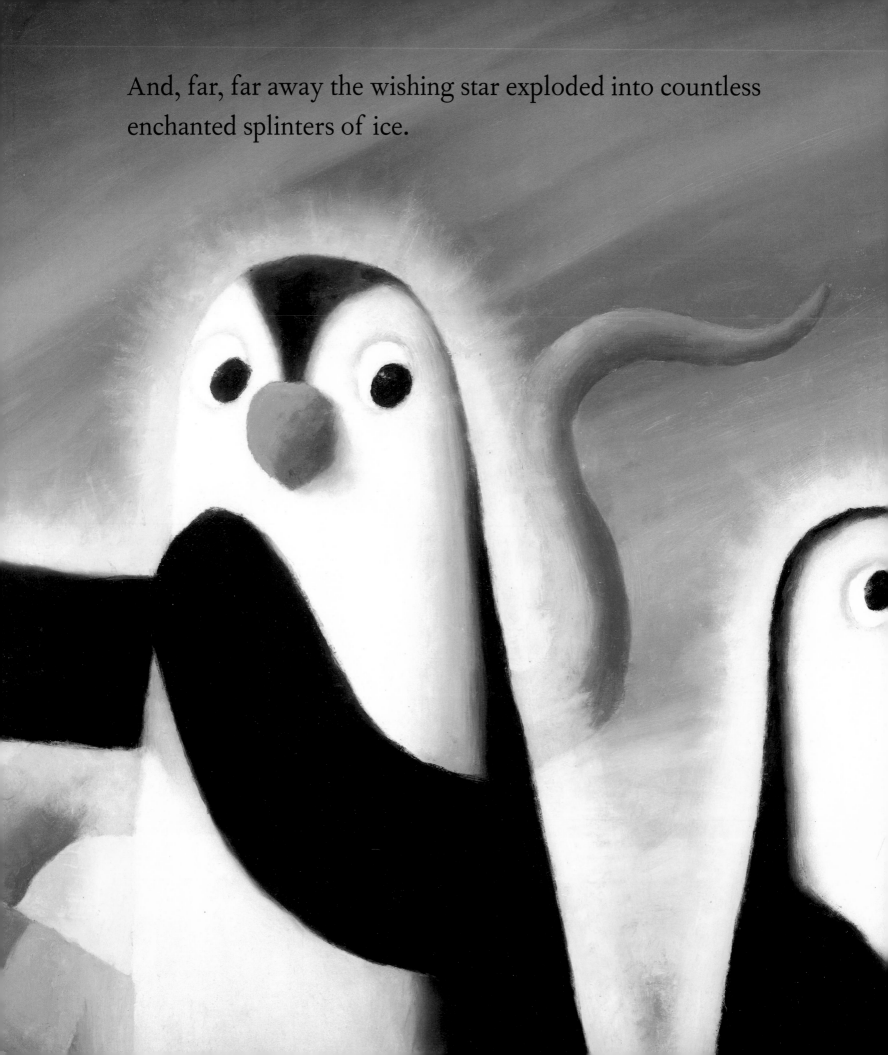

Penguin began to feel very strange.
He was shrinking,
smaller and smaller and smaller.

'Oh no!' gulped little Penguin. 'I'd better run!'

Things would have turned out very
badly for Penguin if Polar Bear and
Miki hadn't appeared with their ice cannon.

'Over here, Penguin!' cried Miki.
'10-9-8-7-6-5-4-3-2-1 — FIRE!'

The monsters were frozen to the spot.

'Wheeee! Thank you!' squealed all the little
penguins. 'Now we've got a winter wonderland
of our very own. Come back soon and play!'

'That was an exciting birthday,'
said Penguin, when they got home.
'What shall we wish for next year?
Superpowers? I'll be the fastest
penguin in the world. Let's...'

'But first,' said Miki, 'I'm going to make my birthday wish.

Starlight, moonshine, ice and snow,
I wish that our friendship
will always grow.
Through darkest night,
whatever may be,
We'll stay together,
just us three.'

'...go to bed now,' yawned Polar Bear.

And a million miles away,
a wishing star exploded in
a shower of sparks.

Miki smiled sleepily. 'Night Penguin.
Night Polar Bear.'

'Night night Miki,' said Polar Bear.
But Penguin was already fast asleep,
racing through the stars in his dreams.

To Mum and Dad

First published in hardback in 2012 by Hodder Children's Books
Copyright © Stephen Mackey 2012

WWW.STEPHENMACKEY.COM

Hodder Children's Books, 338 Euston Road, London, NW1 3BH
Hodder Children's Books Australia, Level 17/207 Kent Street, Sydney, NSW 2000

A catalogue record of this book is available from the British Library.

HB ISBN 978 1 4449 0136 8

Printed in China

Hodder Children's Books is a division of Hachette Children's Books,
an Hachette UK Company

WWW.HACHETTE.CO.UK